SCRUPLE TALES

Scruple Tales
Edited & Compiled by Vidurshi Majithia
Print Edition

First Published in India in 2021
Inkfeathers Publishing
New Delhi 110095

ISBN 978-93-90882-25-0

www.inkfeathers.com

SCRUPLE TALES

Edited & Compiled by

Vidurshi Majithia

Inkfeathers Publishing

DISCLAIMER

The anthology "Scruple Tales" is a collection of 4 Short Stories, 36 Poems and 9 Flash Fiction by 28 authors who belong to different parts of the globe.

The anthology editor and the publisher have ensured to make the content as reader-friendly and plagiarism-free as possible. Unless otherwise indicated, all the names, characters, objects, businesses, places, events, incidents- whether physical/non-physical, real/unreal, tangible/ intangible in whatsoever description used in this book are either the product of the author's imagination or used in a fictitious manner. Any resemblance to actual persons, objects, entities, living or dead, or actual events is purely coincidental.

The stories, poems and flash fictions published in this book are solely owned by their respective authors and are in no way intended to hurt anyone's religious, political, spiritual, brand, personal or fanatic beliefs and/or faith, whatsoever.

In case, any sort of plagiarism is detected in the stories, poems or flash fictions within this anthology or in case of any complaints or grievances or objections, neither the anthology editor nor the publisher is to be held responsible.

CO-AUTHORED BY

Jaykumar Patel | Ben Holdeman | Aakriti Jain

Shravastee Bhattacharya | Juwairiyah Tariq Sayeed

Ujjwal Dutta | Jagruthi Kommuri | Saba Shaikh

Pradip Chauhan | Nandish Bhayani | Akshata Rai

Riet Dsilva | Priyanka Goswami | Bushra Tahir

Sarthak Khurana | Christina Choudhary

Chirag Sumesara | John Jason Thomas | Shradha Patnaik

Aeiknor Kaur | Sonali Mistry | Gunjan Makhijani

Siddiqua Fatima | Rashi Jain | Neeraj Bhengra

Ankita Baidya | Iniya Sisodia | Vidurshi Majithia

CONTENTS

MEET THE EDITOR

Vidurshi Majithia

She breathes hope and exhales poetry. A love-believer, optimist and animal-lover who dreams about inspiring people. She is a physics graduate, a spoken English and soft skills trainer, Writer, Editor, and Poet who loves expressing her philosophical views on life and human emotions while being a voracious reader who learns from every little thing in the Universe.

EDITOR'S NOTE

I have always believed that there is a very thin line, between growing into a protagonist and an antagonist, and that life and suffering is all dazzling theatre, waiting for you to embrace yourself and bring out the real you. We, as humans, are grey creatures and we have always had moments, which left us at an empty barren land. Most of us would have two roads diverging into different realities and the one we choose chooses who we shall be.

We can either take the one of Hope, trust, love, kindness, empathy and realisation, while holding back to our moral values and roots, enlightening our paths and elevating our souls. Or we can take the one of dissatisfaction, emotional dependency, greed, anger and revenge, leading us to some dark bushes, wandering to nowhere. There is suffering in both, but the one we choose makes us what we shall become!

Keeping that in mind, I have compiled this book with poetry, fiction and stories from humans all over the globe and have enveloped their experiences, grey and real into this portable magic that you are holding. Some stories are inspired by humans and their experiences while some humans are inspired by stories, and I think the cycle is never-ending hence it goes on!

With these ravishing writers and the voice their words carry, I want you to glance at your life and take a journey to your conscience, with space for realisation and empathy, embracing what you find and enveloping it into your soul and giving birth to Miracles, because you know the light is within you and so is the darkness!

I hope that you find a new self and that this book succeeds in inspiring you.

Vidurshi Majithia

SCRUPLE TALES

1

WHAT AFTER DEATH?

by Vidurshi Majithia

The days seem blurred,
even the nights are gloomy.
How strange would you feel
when life takes away from you,
That one thing, you were always proud of?
That one person you always believed in
That one emotion in the entire universe, for which
you could put your soul and heart together
Is this what they call being depressed?
Or perhaps being broken or hollow!
When every path you could see
is lost between the dreary thoughts
of the future and past.
When you would search the world
to find yourself, but could nowhere find it.
All you would be left with

would be a dark, stray creature.

That day you should pick a piece at once,
and gather these scraps into a renaissance.
That day you should leave all your pain
for the holy Earth to swallow,
and breathe harder to fill in the Universe inside you.
You shall collect back all your roots
that defined you and your conscience.
You shall sacrifice all the dark left inside,
for the nights to turn into dawns.

You shall build back hope and positivity,
and fill your veins with all the love
the universe has to give you.
You shall create for the world,
a new character and a new life.
You should live it with all honesty.
You should keep building it up.
You should rise high up to the sun.
You should reach wide until the horizon.

Because, sometimes healing is not enough.
You need to be reborn.

2
WHITE SMOKE

by Vidurshi Majithia

Like breath it entered my body, touching the depths of my vessels.

Digging out the darkness inside me.

The white smoke mixed up so well with the air, just like life mixes up with death.

Slowly taking out my soul, introducing me to the darkness inside me...

I couldn't cry but just puff a few more of that stick and sigh, “He loved me! It was just the distance which brought along misunderstandings, then there were some unseen efforts, and a room for ego and lack of communication. It wasn’t meant to happen, it happened because I didn’t understand him.

It wasn’t him, who left me helpless to forget about that nine-year-old bond. It was my own darkness.” mumbled my brain.

And then, the white smoke went out of my nostrils, full of all the darkness within me, high up to heaven...

To tell my stories to him.

3

DARKNESS

by Aakriti Jain

As I raised my hands
gently placing my palm
to feel the warmth of your presence
inside the vacated room, all I could find
was a continuous record playing
of a cinema.

As I moved my feet with pointed heels,
my hands stretching to the most,
creating a muse on that repeated glitched voice:
"You can dance."

But I was not aware of where the voice seeped in...
Or was it just a hallucination?
I could smell the scented flowers,

It usually happens during pujas in Calcutta.
No; they did not allow me to dance,
but I could...

I danced within four walled spaces,
I could have escaped from this eerie night,
and I tried to hitch.

But they couldn't drag me down,
'cause my passion burnt alive!

4

WINGS AND CHAINS

by Nandish Bhayani

Somewhere between psychological theories and
hunting for defects in the system,
she lost it.

The passion she carried,
the love she had for her life
was taken away by some bizarre incidents.

All she could see were flashes.
Some dark, some darker and some dreadful.
The discern of feeling her ashes
enfeebling her towards her extremity.

The fear of failure,
that once, did not have the courage to touch her,
started to choke her to incontinence.

And the pressure,
made her bury her own self alive.
Where she could neither feel the heat of the sand
nor her dispersed soul.

And her tomb,
instead of spelling her name and time stamp,
yelled her location precisely.

"On the cliff where Hope diminished"

5

WILLOW TREE

by Shravastee Bhattacharya

Somedays I feel like dying and being caged away in
a willow tree, with no one to brood over my past
predicament.
Will you be the one to lament for me?

Will you shed those tears like pearl droplets hanging
on to that leaf, drenched in the dew of sunshine of the
red sun on a cool breezy morning sea?

Will I be remembered for my pen with which I wrote
poetry of a broken beat, if someday i feel like dying
and being caged in a willow tree?

Will my reciprocal human beings ever think about me,
Will they remember my smile that I used to hide?
Or will they remember the worst of me?

Will my mother, whom I love the most, cry the most
and call for me, or will she turn as empty as ever just as
me? Will I be cherished finally when someday I would feel
like dying and being caged away in a willow tree?

These worldly connections, the ties, the emotions behind,
they all give me aspirations someday to be selfish for me,
for my father who has always supported me, for my
mother who has always loved me unconditionally.

Somedays I feel like dying and being caged away in a
willow tree but for my people I'll thrive to be the best of
me.

6

WINGS

by Bushra Tahir

I was floating amongst the clouds,
but my feet seemed to have been injured.
I saw a tree hugely dense.
How should I filter through the branches?
Oh I am a bird, I can scan my way in.

She had tenderly swung me upwards
and I clutched the sharp air with my infant wings,
when a wild flock hindered my path
and I lost my grip on the wind.
Would I learn to survive this vastness?
Or would I become this ruthless?

The softness of your body fades to nothing
if the spirit is determined to live.
Let your wings hold both the beauty of a feather and the vigour of a metal.
Don't be afraid of the heaviness,
you can still soar high.

7

JOY OF THE SUNRISE

by Jaykumar Patel

Early at the morning sunrise, when I got out of the bed,
the moments suddenly started to whisper.
Running with wild gallops, it wasn't a normal day.
Fewer were the slogans not so long to last,
'cause, I started remembering the happiness of the past.
Stumbling on the balcony with a beautiful breeze,
With thoughts of wonder all over my head,
I felt power within my veins which were earlier 'dead'.

I realized that I was living in vain, seeing the beauty in 'remains'.
I forgot my pain and started overcoming the drain.
I realized that there is more in life, still left to be heard and done.
I gathered my toolkit and found my point of stay;

Where my passion lies, where my mind fights and heart wins with fewer tries.

I felt the door swinging back and forth coming to a pause and was now opened for me to jump and surf in the snow

At night, I came back again to that place.

Travelled a lot inside, knowing the gains and sorrows I faced.

I was happy that I had so much more than before.

I heard my voice and silenced the noise.

Because I realized, that though I loved

to wear a colour as black as the night,

The days are always going to be bright and white!

So fight, endure yourself and roll over all favourable dice.

Because one day you will surely experience the joy of the Sunrise!

8

BORN AGAIN

by Ben Holdeman

Clearing of the eyes
Settled the debts of yesterday's life
Bypassing any final goodbyes
They had their time
Strengthened the soul inside
Stopped believing the critic's lies
Let that die
Watched the phoenix rise
I'm finally alive

9

MEMORIES OF MISERY

by Chirag Sumesara

Part 1: The Studio

"LIGHTS...CAMERA...SOUND ROLL AND ACTION!"

That's how my story started.

My dad got a job at a film studio and we were happy because now at least we had a roof over our head.

Growing up in a film studio was an uncanny adventure. We were studio cleaners, who lived in the studio for free. We saw things that we could have never imagined. But fortune came to my doorstep when the studio approached me to cast me as a child actor in a film. Everybody was happy except my dad.

Let me tell you about us. We were four siblings, two brothers and two sisters, and I was the eldest girl and dad's most favourite.

So, when they came to offer me a child actor's role, he rejected it straight away as he loathed the film Industry.

One day my uncle secretly took me to another film set and told me that I would be on TV. I was cast as a child actor for a 3-minute role. When my dad came to know about this, he beat the shit out of my uncle. Later, my role was chopped off.

Part 2: The Struggle

Life constantly reminded us about our condition and we had to find some other way to gather money, not for food, not for our school or rent, but for drinking water. My mom despised the condition we were living in, and I was her least favourite, the reason is still a mystery. My Dad was a man of his words, he used to get a lot of respect from everyone but that doesn't settle the bills, right?

Four days of discarded food from the studio made us nauseous, but we couldn't afford to get sick. It's a mystery that when everything collapses when hope dies, you get a silver lining that turns your life around.

Within a week, dad found another job that would redeem our lives. But that didn't last as people came knocking on our tent to ask for money. I was an 8-year-old who had never seen a coloured TV or film despite them being shot in front of us.

Debt was piling up, and Dad slipped into depression. Now whatever he earned was squandered on alcohol or drugs.

I still remember my mom humiliating my dad for his addiction. Later he took me out when everyone was sleeping and for the first time I saw him crying, and after that what he said still echoes in my ear, "Never trust this family of ours." Later he gave me ice cream!

The next morning, there was a lot of commotion in the studio. Maybe a big star would be coming on set so I didn't check. Little did I know that it was not a big film star but the pieces of my dad's dead body rolled up in a blanket.

Part 3: The Eldest

I still don't know what pushed my dad into jumping in front of a train in broad daylight. The police advised us not to see the condition of his dead body. Now we were alone, or maybe it was just me.

Being the eldest, I was expected to step up. Even if that meant dropping from school, or leaving my entire childhood to help my family survive.

I dropped out of school. Mom was working twice a day to put food on the table and I was working in the studio as a cleaner.

I was handling everything! From beating the shit out of my younger brothers for skipping school to taking care of them like a mom. It's funny that we all were kids, but I was the chosen one who had to sacrifice everything. Now I was a 30-year-old living inside the body of a 17-year-old but things were about to change.

My mom constantly reminded me of how disgusting my father was and that I had a lot of him in me. Sometimes they would lock me inside the house so that all of them can go for a picnic as a "family". Confined in the darkness, all I could think of were my father's last words "Don't trust this family of ours," and I guess he was right.

The next day, I finished my work and came home. My Aunt approached me with a gigantic smile, and what she said next gave me chills. "Congratulations! Your mom has fixed your marriage!"

Part 4: The Marriage

Marriage is supposed to be an entwinement of two souls, not a deal between families. I didn't even know the name of the guy I was going to spend my entire life with. But one of my cousins helped me to get in touch with the boy. Later we planned a meeting, let's just call it a date. So, with an anxious heart, wearing a borrowed dress, I went to see him.

Surprisingly the guy turned out to be a gentleman with a perfect sense of humour. Our conversation went till evening, and then I had to get back before anyone would know. But it was already dark, we were miles away from my place, and I had no money with me.

"Should I drop you to the cab?" he asked.

"Nah, I prefer walking, care to join?"

"Umm…Sure!"

And we walked 17 km.

My marriage was a long movie without an interval. All I remember was someone throwing some coloured powder on my face. Most of which went through my nose to the throat and soon I was rushed to the hospital.

The doctor used some jargon to explain my situation, but I couldn't register anything. I told him to explain it to me in a layperson's language.

"Your lungs are damaged. Although nothing serious, when your body is under stress you might get Asthma."

These words were enough for me to know the seriousness of the situation. And a few months later, I was pregnant.

Part 5: The Miracle

Miracles do happen, that's what everyone says, but I wasn't lucky enough to witness it happening until now. I felt that pregnancy would be the only time when everyone was so concerned about me. I enjoyed the bit of attention, but that later turned into the pressure of giving birth to a boy.

I was so frantic that if I had the power to determine the gender of my child, maybe I would.

Finally, the day arrived, and I went into labour. Nobody told me how painful it would be. But then it all ended, a child was born, and to my surprise, it was a boy.

After a while my breathing got heavy and I lost my consciousness. I vividly remember how nobody asked how I was doing, as if the sole reason for my existence was to give birth to a baby boy.

The doctor came in with some reports and with a concerned look he uttered 3 words that would change everything, "You have Asthma."

I cried for hours.

Part 6: The Change

Watching your kids grow is an experience that is more precious than finding God. But I wasn't fortunate enough to experience this joy; I spent most of my time working. I had to work 6 hours then come home, do household chores, and prepare meals for 10 people. Many times, I faced difficulty in breathing and had to keep a machine that the doctor provided me, which was my life machine. I had no idea what my child was doing. I never got to play with him or spend some time with him. I didn't even know if his first words were "Mama".

I kept my asthma a secret. My husband turned out to be a workaholic and alcoholic. He was a responsible husband and an obedient son, but he was also what we call an "Absent father".

When it was my boy's 5th birthday, I completed my job early so I could celebrate with him. But when I reached home, I saw bruises on his face, cheeks scratched and nose bleeding. He was bullied because he had spectacles for his low vision.

His friends constantly harassed him for being timid. The teacher regularly scolded him because he was a slow learner.

This is not something you accept your child to go through. I took the matter into my own hands and started teaching him the basics in the night. I used to ask a favour from people who knew English to teach me some, so I could later teach that to my kid. Watch some motivational videos and narrate to him to boost up his morals.

I would pick discarded books from the trash to tell him stories. And I guess this little effort had a butterfly effect.

It's been decades since I had started a business of my own and my boy is doing wonders. Maybe what I experienced helped me build a person who would later grow up and change my world and take me to places where I had never been, and be present for me.

Now I'm old and I can't wait for my grandchildren to ask about my story and I would say,
"LIGHTS...CAMERA...SOUNDROLL AND ACTION!"

10

JUST A PHASE

by Saba Shaikh

My heart is wrenched.
My soul is drenched.
Does this agony even have an end?

Trembling hands.
Dreading fear.
I have been, for peace, all my life dear.

Restless days.
Sleepless nights.
But I hope it's just a phase and not my life!

11

AM I STRONG OR WEAK?

by Jagruthi Kommuri

Am I strong or am I weak?
These feelings I feel so intense to keep,
Maybe I'm weak to feel so strong,
Or maybe I'm strong but it feels so wrong,
Maybe I'm weak cause sometimes I weep,
But yes, I'm strong, I smile when it hurts deep.

Are you weak? Or are you strong?
Those feelings dearly to you belong.
No matter what bitter or sweet,
They depend only on how you treat,
Maybe life is just like a song,
We may forget the lyrics; the rhythm remains lifelong.

12

A FALLEN LEAF

by Akshata Rai

I was walking on the sound of leaves crushing
under my feet
yellow and brownish
after burning in the sun
and dancing in the wind
were now fallen down
lying on the ground
ready to bury themselves up.
I picked up a leaf
and held it on my palm,
and for some odd reason
it looked like I knew it.
The lines and veins on it
reflected the creases on my palm
the lines on my palm

narrates my story.
Is that the same reason why leaves have veins scribbled on them?

Listen,
or read, or just watch
and the leaves will have a story to tell.

The story of a day when the storm was too strong
and the leaf on the edge of breaking
but it didn't
and the storm passed away.
A story of the night when it stayed awake and watched the bud bloom into a flower
a story I'd say, the day when it hid behind another leaves
in search of shadow and shelter
because the rain was too hard to take.
A story of the day when it's freedom from the tree
wasn't the end of its life
but the beginning of a new one
from my palm
to in between the pages of my book.

13

THE GLASS CHILD

by Riet Dsilva

To you, the world, I truly say,
you're nothing but all deceit and lies,
all I had you took away.
Now there's no one here to apologize.

The nights though warm, they terrify,
Overwhelming fear comes creeping in too.
The heart and mind no more agree,
All because I favoured you.

The dark within is raging now.
The hateful screams ravage my soul,
in all my attempts to fight it somehow,
I fall prey to your vengeful control.

I'm a moving crypt, my soul encased.
I struggle to find my time and space.
The doors to peace are open wide,
yet I can't seem to step inside.

I foresee the dark revived,
that feasts and feeds on innocent beings,
mistreated, misplaced a pitied glass child.
All knowing and all seeing.

The wasteland of my earliest thoughts
is far and now will never nearer be.
Others have wandered in and out,
but somehow all of them have failed to see.

It's a battlefield and I'm trapped inside,
no place to go, no place to hide.
I'm trying to fix what I've done wrong,
and find a place where I belong.
Then soon I'll find what I lack,
and self-love will change me back.

14

THE MONK AND A GIRL

by Gunjan Makhijani

A girl asked a monk,

"How do I know if I love that person?"

"At what level can you go just to know this?"

"Just put the amount. It will be in your pocket. I promise."

"You don't have to worry. I won't ask you for money. I don't charge anyone," the monk replied.

“Okay. Then, what will I have to do?”

"It's not that simple," he said.

"You say and I will do it," the girl replied confidently.

"You have your mother at your home?"

"Yes."

"Imagine you are at her funeral."

The girl was startled.

Her wide eyes and open mouth conveyed that she had not been expecting this.

But since she had promised that she would do anything to know if she truly loved that person, she had to follow what the monk would say.

"Imagine your mother is dead in front of you."

"I... I can't."

"But you promised that you would do anything."

The girl glanced in the eyes of the monk. Never in her dreams she thought a monk would act this way.

"I did," she said after a few minutes.

"What did you see"'

"I was sobbing very hard."

"On whose shoulder?"

"I didn't see."

"Place someone's shoulder. Of whom it would have been?"

"The one who will be with me, in the darkest situations, the one who will support me."

"Are you able to imagine that person's shoulder, about whom you are unsure whether you love him or not?"

The girl closed her eyes. Soon tears rolled down. Sometimes, some things come inevitably, just like tears.

She opened her eyes.

"I can feel that the shoulder is his."

The monk smiled and said,

"Congratulations, you are in love."

15

SHE

by Sonali Mistry

She poured a glass of whiskey with a cigarette in another hand,
She is crazy, isn't she?
For lighting a fire to burn her parliament.

Mad over those expectations,
She's hungry for all the attention.
Crazy for saving that grievance,
Lustful to ignite her vengeance.

She is stronger to shut the screams,
and vicious for toxic dreams.
Her desire for celebrating a funeral
is exotic enough to attract you, a sinner.

A dark and black livery to host,

the wine with jellyfish on toast.
Those juicy red lips to crave,
she wore her sinful soul of rave.

The flames looked like emerald though,
she sparked like a black diamond.
That last sip of her neat, golden drink,
she took a small smoke and winked.

Her green eyes were opened,
to see that luxurious grave treat.
She had a little smirk on her face,
to remember all your deeds.

16

LIVING AS A PHOENIX

by Juwairiyah Tariq Sayeed

"On your mark… Get set…" and the whistle blew and I tore through the field for the tenth time in a row.

I just knew that I would be taking part in the 34th NATIONAL JUNIOR ATHLETICS CHAMPIONSHIPS, 2018 when I saw the coach smile looking at the stopwatch.

I sang to myself as I waited for the signal to turn green. My parents would be overjoyed when I'd share the news of my selection with them. I was going to be the youngest to ever participate in this event. I started cycling as soon as the traffic signal gave directions.

I had barely crossed the road when out of the corner of my eyes I saw the blazing headlights of a speeding car and the next thing I know is I'm thrown down the road and then everything went blank.

I opened my eyes to the beeping of machines and found myself lying in a hospital bed. I could feel my entire body burning in a frozen state. My eyes travelled down my length and my world just went numb when the doctor said that I had paraplegia and my legs would no longer be able to support me.

I stayed in bed for days, refused meal after meal and lost my voice. I sank deeper into a den. The wheelchair in the corner of my room sent chills down my spine while it mocked all my dreams and future plans. A life where I was a torment to myself and everyone around me was in sight. I closed my eyes hoping that when I opened them, I would be in the world of eternal peace.

I woke up to find my coach sitting on the chair across my bed. On seeing me awake he came up and uttered to me "Get off the bed, it's not the apocalypse. That day was a bad one but today is a new day. Birds with broken legs can fly as long as they don't let their wings get clipped. The three-day State-level Para Games will be organized by the Karnataka Sports Association next year." and he turned around and left.

It took every ounce of my strength to pull myself together and crawl to the wheelchair. I stared at it, boring a hole through it, wondering if it could help build me a new home over the one razed to the ground. I climbed onto the wheelchair and steered myself out of the front gate and called for my mother's company as I headed to the training field. I worked my fingers to the bone and pushed myself for an extra mile day after day. Every day was a hurdle that I crossed to dig the foundation of this new today deeper.

The ghost of yesterday pumped extra adrenaline as I tore through the track, completing lap after lap. I laid down the cornerstone of my castle as I flew with the ribbon into bliss. I looked around at the cheering crowd, my coach and my parents as tears rolled down my cheeks.

That day as I held onto the gold medal, I addressed the millions who were trapped in the calamity of life and said,

"In flames, I saw myself burn,

And from ashes, I saw rebirth.

On the ruins of Carthage, Rome was built.

When you break is when you get to relive to rebuild."

17

I'LL KEEP ROWING

by Neeraj Bhengra

Miles away from being under the dome,
one loveful call and I'll be home.
Days go and nights come and always they turn,
behind the bars, my life is summed.
I got soaked whilst navigating the sea,
sleeping on the dirt, let my skeleton rest,
out are they, stars and moon,
my prayer to Christ is to meet you soon.

Laying down, under the same dark sky,
my promise was not a lie.
Believe in the cross around your neck,
whilst my life shakes.
I know it's impossible amidst this cruel time
but I'll keep the light of hope glowing.
It might take a thousand days,

Until I reach you, I'll keep rowing.

18

UNENDING GRIEF

by Christina Choudhary

Hide and seek with my thoughts,
winning and losing was its part,
winning filled me with immense glee,
losing was not what I want.

One day I lost and was caught.
Weapons to fight failed to protect.
Slowly and steadily was losing my strength,
and a day came when I couldn't fight.
Thoughts surrounding me
were eating me up.
Soon, I turned hollow from within.
Losing myself day by day
was not less than a death every day.
Amidst my war, there was a man,
who knew everything but his silence said it all,

whose smile said a mystery for us to find.
One day, like an angel he flew away,
carrying my sorrows to where they could come never again.
To give me a new life and hope,
he went to one who can give me both.
Not a mythical creature, he was
my grandfather.
He carried my sorrows and
gave me a reason to live.

19

FLAMES OF PHOENIX

by Infinity Zero

Your words are fleeting,
like the wings of a hummingbird
and I carved my heart out
to mould into your perfect world.
My house of flowers
is buried in the avalanche
of lies and battered fiction,
just an abstract romance.
Wings ablaze, I keep falling,
a descend to the mortal world
but I'll rise again like a phoenix
from the ashes of my burning soul.

20

THE GHOST AND THE PHOENIX

by Ben Holdeman

Left my life in a mystery
Strummed my heart with a memory
Locked inside a fever dream
Guess you knew what you did to me

Ripped this heart from my chest
Threw it in a pile with all the rest
Walk through life like you are blessed
In this reality you infest

Found my way back to me
Lifted myself to my feet
Let go of this misery
The strength inside supersedes

21

SO BEGIN AGAIN

by Jaykumar Patel

Dead things are never reborn,
they are reproduced in mere prejudice;
This could be the lame world where not everyone is wise,
so, begin again and ignore the lies.

Diversity in its vein, still juggling in the 'past' with remorse gains,
moving apart from the guilt of present names,
so, begin again, and overcome this fame.

Truth wins and love never faints, no matter how much heavily it rains,
but sometimes it comes in the saddest domain.
So, begin again to get away from this pain.

If it's not the time, then wait for the perfect rhyme,
maybe someday you will learn to play this flowering divine,
so, begin again, and master this showering game.

Dead things are never reborn, they are reproduced with several mocking gates,
fearing is not an option to deal with this rewarded fate,
Therefore, begin again, and ride without any wait.

22

CHASING THE RAINBOWS, DYING EMPTY

by Aeiknor Kaur

'Orange' is all the sunsets in your eyes,
for days you laugh more than you smile,
and smile more than you should.

'Purple' is a hint of magic in everything,
for days of luck and belief in 'touch woods'.

'Blue' is the taste and smell of longing for rain,
nights when it's the skies that cry when your eyes cannot.

'Red' is the relief of a wrist you've cut,
distraction from the pain of all your dreams gone to rot.

'Green' is the beauty of a four leafed clover,
new dreams you forged from old pains.

'Yellow' is the sun kissed sand on beaches,
for the days your bones are gold,
and you have ichor in your veins.

'Pink' is the blush of a smile,
and secret kisses from your lover.

'Grey' is a smell of smoke and hell,
and you walk out of it just a little bit tougher.

'Black' is blood from a broken heart,
a quintessential end to a rendezvous.

'White' is for purity, poetry and falling snowflakes,
all things beautiful that make you, you.

And I hope, when you die,
there is a rainbow over your grave,
I hope you live so much,
that in death there's nothing of you left to save.
And trophies, money, nothing matters, because don't you see?
It's colours we give and take,
colours that define us,
and I pray, for our sakes,
That we all die empty.

23

THE UNSEEN POETRY OF EVERYDAY LIFE

by Shradha Patnaik

Hello there!

Now you may have wondered why this person has titled something so philosophical and maybe to some it may seem a bit pretentious and let me say I felt the same until I finished writing this directionless piece. I hope I can convince you of the title and maybe at the end we can agree on some point. Fingers crossed.

So, I am a 19-year-old person and I refer to myself as a person rather than gender first because in the hierarchical context of my conscience I prefer myself as a human being rather than all the alphabetical F/M labels of male or female or LGBTQ.

Emotions make us human, don't they?

In 2018, I finally reached the pinnacle of Exam stress aka Universal syndrome of Exam Fear aka Science 12th CBSE finals.

Now, to prepare for that you need months and I barely studied in the winter holidays. That's when I saw my most vulnerable self and I hate to admit it I needed that phase. To constantly sit and study at my desk and attend coaching classes was gruesome and overwhelming and in my mind, a desert and a storm were creating havoc, the result was pretty much the same as the chain reaction I was studying in Chemistry.

Anxiety, stress, insecurity, fear, these are kind of a package deal. And these types of thoughts turn into variations of dark shades each thought would blight my yellow sunshine of optimism with dark shadows of self-doubt and fear of failure. Thoughts like an army of "what ifs" questions would pop up in my head. What if I forget a topic? What if I am unable to finish the paper on time? What if I fail?

These thoughts were so overwhelming that it would bring a hurricane inside my mind and my head would spin and the room would seem smaller for all my infinite problems. So, I would rush out of the confines of the pale-yellow walls and towards the colourful canvas of nature.

In the month of January, the weather is at its best in Bangalore. And in my mind, there's always mirages in the midst of a desert of stress. That mirage is imagination or fantasies. I often use my imagination as a vehicle for escaping the shackles of everyday stress. And I use music as a button for activating my imagination. And this vehicle of imagination has no bounds just like Hagrid's flying motorcycle. I'd often think of stories to write down after my exams are over. I'd ponder over the possibilities of the character, things that the character can achieve and do, adventures I didn't get to live in real life.

I often think people underestimate the importance of a window, a rooftop or even a balcony. They may seem like very ordinary architecture, but when thinking in terms of mental health they do play a very important role. These structures provide a kaleidoscope of observations that one can often miss due to the daily humdrum of life. But to me, these very ordinary parts of our homes help me to relieve the tension and escape for a little. I would go to the rooftop of my apartment and take a deep breath and look up to the blue sky and soft music playing in my earphones. There's something magical about this process. Watching the shapeless clouds fluttering through the sky is very satisfying. Noticing the pastel shades of orange, blue and purple at sunset.

And after the sunset show and good vibes, the shy entry of bedazzling stars gives a feeling of something good, in Japanese this feeling is called 'Komorebi'- sunlight filtering through the trees. And I would often look around from the top view. The buildings and houses and towards the horizon. I'd observe the people walking in the streets and driving their cars and watering their plants. Somehow looking down, from my ivory tower of anxiety I'd feel a sense of calmness spread through my mind and heart.

There are so many people and each of them have their own problems and stress, and I am also one of them but life goes on. Similarly, I'd come to the realisation when I'd look up to the stars which are light years away from us, my problems would seem infinitesimally smaller like a speck of dust in the air. So, preferably I would take a walk to go to my tuition class. A hardly 10-minute walk under the trees and gardens of the residences and of course soft music playing in my earphones. I skip and sprint in the journey, sometimes I sing along, sometimes I take a longer route to savour the journey, sometimes I try a different road and I often introspect myself especially when it rains. With rain puddling at my feet, I see my own reflection and recheck if that's the real me or not. I sometimes wish we all can come to a standstill moment and count to 1,2,3 and self-actualize our dreams, desires and identity.

So, after taking many walks throughout that year I stopped worrying about the future and started to live in the moment. Instead of locking up that emotional baggage I scattered all of them to the mighty wind. Like a warm blanket on a winter morning. I started appreciating the little things of everyday life, I started reading and writing and photographing these unseen poetry and symphonies of everyday life.

I hope now you understand why I have titled this as mentioned. I really wish you start fine-tuning this unseen poetry in your own unique manner, not for anyone else but yourself.

24

EMBRACE THE SKIN YOU ARE IN

by John Jason Thomas

Embrace the skin you are in
It will make your life better
Vaccinate all your thoughts
and hold them together!
These thoughts would build
Your integrity and define you
Your integrity comes from
what you are, and how you think
So, leaving behind your skin
And trying to transform it isn't wise enough!
Embrace your skin, because it makes unique
Just like every different thing in the Universe.

25

DESPITE

by Rashi Jain

Despite the condemnations I got,
I am still sailing right in the ocean of life.
Despite being called a loser,
I didn't give up the way I think of my future.
Despite being unable to answer them back
I know that I am right and they are wrong somewhere.
Despite being odd in those even brilliants,
my heart and mind are in perfect coordination.
Despite being bullied by my own ones
I know I am superior in forgiveness somewhere.
Despite being subjected to millions of harsh comments,
I always tried to forget them crying a billion moments.
Despite always being made a laughing stock,
I tried to cool my mind and take a walk somewhere
Despite always being the one crying,
I tried to smile knowing my heart's lying somewhere.

Despite being questioned on my every decision,
I tried not to shake on what I had chosen.
Despite being someone undesired by people,
I desired myself thinking they don't deserve my consideration.
Despite being at the bottom of the world,
I tried to capture whatever I saw and heard.

26

SHOWER THOUGHTS | 3 A.M. |

by Aakriti Jain

It was 3:00 a.m.
while I was cleaning 'it'
had cologne over the 'stain'
which reminded me of our last visit.
Being a past-dweller,
I felt "our" memories taking triumph
over my crime.
I aversed with my mind;
If only,
I would have dropped that knife.
That day,
was a concoction of
guilt and solace.
the weather had
in itself the tinch of
"purity" as well as "immorality".

27

HOW WAS YOUR NIGHT

by Bushra Tahir

There are shreds of life falling on the ground, floating in the sky,
people have taken it off their souls
when the silence falls and head rules,
all you think about are those shreds.
Those bits you tore away from you
at that moment, it appears like stars spread across the night,
tempting and unattainable.

Forget about the days for a while,
how was your night?

Did you have a good time socializing?
Did you miss that one person,
or it's the million dreams that kept you awake?

Darkness is haunting for a reason,

the emptiness brings out the human in you,

with all its ups and downs,

with all its imperfections and flaws.

Surprisingly, it's heavenly,

we are not worn out, maybe we just need those pieces back.

Maybe it's time to be charming and to slowly attract those shreds you threw out of you.

28

THE COLOURS

by Ankita Baidya

I've been feeling blue lately. Nothing seems to take side with the yellow. There is an empty void that yearns to be filled, not with red but with amber. Life for me is a play of colours, each of them having a very crucial role. We are just a side effect of oblivion. It is the colour that one leaves behind, reiterates itself through the pages of the past and the assumed to be distant future. Today you might feel a shade of yellow with a pearly white background that awaits to be painted or maybe a shade of blue with grey scenery and black spots. Amber, green, pink with the butterflies and the sun while the ash, sapphire, gloomy hues with the rain and an empty night sky.

While there's a concept of gay and glum colours, there's another thought which completely depends on our choices. Some of us might accept blue to be sorrowful but what if we decide to turn it into bliss? What if you accept all your heartaches and your hardships with a pinch of gold and red?

Sometimes we act as if we have an infinite amount of time, spending it on jealousy, revenge, fury and rage. What I mean is a simple fact of breathing without regrets, content with all the red and pink one can receive in a lifetime.

Whether it's the indigo or the lemon, whether it's pouring or shinning, whether there is fury or affection, whether the desires are true or forgotten, whether it's nothing or everything or whether you are stuck amidst this ache of an eternity;

It is a happy day; it is a happy life!

29

DEAR DEPRESSION

by Sarthak Khurana

Dear Depression,

My sincere apologies for answering you a bit late. Because somewhere, I was lost finding the ways out of the cobweb you tried to put me in. I had been wandering in the deepest routes of the thick forest of blooming hitches and the apprehensions going in my mind. And here I am, confronting you with all my will.

I know you love me a lot. You never leave a chance to influence me and show your affection whenever I feel alone. Earlier as a kid, I never knew who you were. I had just heard about you from the old fogey. They told me how you added to their lives by making them stronger than ever. I never thought I would meet you this early and you would become an indispensable part of my life.

I still remember meeting you for the very first time. Autumn had begun. I expected it to pass away faster because I loved winter more than fall. I couldn't wait any longer to finally get new woollen and sleep in the cosy silk quilt. That season did pass away quite fast, taking away with it the most precious person of my life – My Best Friend. I was sad, lonely.

I thought no one could ever replace him in my life. And that's when I saw you coming. You replaced him. You became my best friend.

You were there with me, day and night. You didn't let me sleep, you didn't let me eat or do anything I wanted to. You behaved just like a loyal companion would do, always staying near to me. Eventually, I started thinking you were subjugating me in every aspect. That was the time I started thinking about how to get rid of you. Then my life changed. I moved on a new path in my life leaving you behind. I made new friends and started an entirely new journey. And I was happy. But somewhere I knew you were loyal from your perspective. You would return someday.

I was right. You did. You did follow me wherever I was going and you did perform your duty as a faithful one would do. You returned. I asked you to move out of my life. I was determined this time I won't let you come back and mislead me again. You have made me think a lot of things I never wanted to. You started ruining my life. All you did was go away and then turn back again sometime. I was tired of watching your pendulum striking my mind back and forth. And yet, you came back again. Moreover, you still dared to intimidate me to my worst.

You know what, I am glad you were there. You showed me my worth. You showed me what I was capable of doing. You showed me my weakest points so that I could amend them to my best. And I thank you for it. You've done so much for me that no one else could have done.

This time, I am sure I don't want you in my life anymore. I have those people in my life for whom I can die, those people for whom I can lose my happiness just to see them smile. And you dear depression, thank you for not making me any stronger. Thank you for making me realize how strong I already was. Thanks for making me realize the true worth of my life and the people who make it worth living for me.

Regards,

The Stronger Me

30

POSITIVITY OF LIFE

by Pradip Chauhan

Life is like the rays of sun,
on quiet days with luminous blue skies.
In default, life can be the drop of rain,
that drops off like tears coming from your eyes.
Life can be the paradise,
that you only get through hell,
because you won't know how blessed you are,
if you haven't been sad as well.
Life will teach you a hard lesson,
but you'll be clever once you know,
that even lotus needs both sunshine,
and a touch of rain to grow.

31

HOPE

by Saba Shaikh

Hope is the little thing
that I will always stick to.
Do you think I am stupid?
Well, it's only because of it
that I am living up to
into the darkest forest
upon the strangest street.
It helps me to persist
to fight all my enemies.
Do you think I am infatuated?
But you never know
deep down inside you
you are still living with that little hope.

32

HERE WE GO AGAIN

by Iniya Sisodia

All those gates,
now wide open.
All those memories
now cemented deep inside.
All packed up
down to the last brick.
Came the call
no one deemed worth the wait
ready to be torn down again.
Answering the last bait
only to be built back up again
and I hear myself say
here we go again.

33

SECOND-HAND LIFE

by Ben Holdeman

Did you stop and see?
Did you run and flee?
Living life so vicariously
Watching the world as it bleeds
While your fellow man pleads
As though a show on television
Comforted with the thought
It could never happen to me

34

THE BEST COMPLIMENT

by Siddiqua Fatima

There was a house different from the others. Girls here were pampered, protected and valued. This wasn't the case in other houses in that day and age, nowhere in that land at least. It was the norm to want a son, to praise him and value him, to see perfection in him. But this house was different. In fact, it was heard that this household believed that the greatest blessing from the universe was a daughter. They always hoped that their firstborns would be daughters.

It is rumoured that in one generation of this family, about a hundred years ago, they went on having children till they were blessed with a daughter. They ended up with a few too many sons in that generation, they never wanted so many. In those circumstances and those times though, they didn't mind it that much, the sons helped with the income, with the patriarch making only ten rupees a month any support was appreciated from within the family, financial support from anywhere else would ruin the patriarch's reputation. After all their youngest had to be given the best of everything, she deserved it. Things went on just fine.

Skipping to a more recent timeframe, this family still loves its daughters more. The firstborns in this generation are all daughters, in the previous generation too. They had a few sons as well. There was a balance now in the number of daughters and sons. The daughters always came first, in privilege and in birth too, thankfully they said. Their ancestors smile at them, having returned to the universe, they ensure that the family is always as well-treated as their daughters. The family, despite their non-conforming behaviour, was well respected in society and never lacked anything from the material world. Fortune seemed to seek them out from the rest and as they were blessed with daughters, so they were with everything else.

This family's tradition was that the daughters were the first to be served food, the first to take their pick from anything that had to be shared among the children and the first to get their gifts when anyone returned from a trip. Sometimes, if the person returning from a trip fell short on time to get things for people back home, they would grab something for the daughters at least.

The daughters did learn how to do things, like the girls in other houses, but at their own pace, just to ensure they wouldn't be disadvantaged in any situation. They weren't responsible to get things done; such demands weren't made of them. Daughters were taught to care and love, to cook, for nourishing everyone was an honour there, not a chore that was avoided or disliked. They would be asked to make decisions for the daughters were lucky, even bad decisions yielded good results if made by them.

All sorts of justifications were given for this preference of daughters in this house. All valid too. The daughters were to go off to another house and spend the rest of their lives there.

They knew what society was like, would the daughters ever be treated well? Wasn't it right for them to get everything in the beginning so they could give for the rest of their lives after that? The sons would stay. They would be able to get what they didn't initially. With time things would balance. But in the house where they are born, daughters would come first, always.

Time passed, there was chaos, and turmoil in the world around them, people were losing livelihoods and the economy was failing, politics corrupting. Even with fortune on their side, things were hard. By then the children grew up, some moved out, some stayed. It so happened that just a daughter had remained at home. Having been raised in comfort, and with love and care, she was in no hurry to leave. With time on her hand and nothing much to do, she offered to do the chores and lend a hand with the errands. She did all she was taught a daughter was to do. She was supportive and helpful, happy and kind, dedicated and enthusiastic.

As a daughter, she was well appreciated too. The elders valued her more than they always did, they treasured her and praised her, told her they were proud of how she was independent and still knew how to look after others. Truly she was an ideal child. She was so perfect in every way, she was a son! No better compliment could be found for the qualities she possessed. All those present agreed. She was a son indeed.

35

A CHILD IS BORN YET KILLED

by Jagruthi Kommuri

A child is born in a world full of hate,
he grows up clueless about his fate,
as he learns to take a step and slowly run,
he loses his childhood that can never return.
All of the implications of world to satisfy,
he is left with only doubts, fears and cries,
in a world where his voice isn't heard,
he is forced to be silent and slurred.
As he tries to find solutions to his unanswered questions,
he is only disappointed and left in depression,
though he learns there's freedom of expression,
but only as much accepted by the world of impression.
Nowhere does he find people kind and wise,
but is surrounded by all idiots and vice.
Every day a child is born at the same time being killed,
in a world of hatred and obsession, let kindness be rebuilt.

A child needs to know that there's still love and hope,
in the world that is destroyed, there's little scope to cope.
So, let's all make this world a kind and better place,
to every dying child in a human let there be grace to embrace.

36

DEAR MIND

by Neeraj Bhengra

Dear mind,
I know you like to play games with me,
and manipulate the subjects that we see.
You convince me to believe in things that aren't true.
I know you like to create illusions,
but the only thing you create in me is confusion.
You overthink, over care, and over love,
but that only gives birth to anxiety in me.
You make me obsessed with certain things,
and compel me to achieve those imaginary wings.
You make me perform rituals,
and love to mess with my visuals.
You kept forcing me to reassure,
that my preciouses is holy and safe.

Trust me, I'm sure.

Oh dear, you are so insecure,
but I have to do something to get cured.
You are like the angry sea during the day,
giving me false alarms.
At night, you become like the silent sea,
You are in so much peace and calm.
Your peace became my obsession,
So, you compelled me to sleep forever.
I was on the verge of fulfilling your wish,
But I could not and will not.
Neither am I a coward nor am I afraid.
You are slowly killing my cheerful soul.
Yet I'm not losing hope.
I know I will be okay.

Just fine, for now.
But my soul will be happy again.
This is a dark and scary night.
But I have faith, a new day will begin.

37

FIREFLIES

by Infinity Zero

Imprisoned in the catacombs of despair
I feel my world crumbling down, bit by bit,
my heart mourned the loss of the sun
as you walked away, leaving only fear.
I find my peace under the starry skies
my dark heart, slowly turn stelliferous,
a firefly glowing bright, I illuminate.
Even in melancholy, I find myself again.

38

ONCE UPON A TIME IN LOCKDOWN

by Jaykumar Patel

Let's go and move on
untimely this lockdown will be gone!
We studied or not,
the webinars were a lot.
Fighting for an immiscible thought
eating food like a harvesting knot.
Tidy is the weather, untidy our arms,
roaming in the evenings, the terrace - Amsterdam.
With 10000 touches a day on the bluest screen
eyes on movies and documentaries - a highest esteem.
Some used to read and some made us learn,
some jumped to cook and some had a treat.
Some amused to sing and some used to dance
to gather at a place was merely a chance.
Chatting and chanting always an open door
TikTok and media, fun with games indoors.

Through the vicinity of pain and an urge to freedom,

through a wisp of rage and a lot of boredom.

We never stopped learning; we never stopped dreaming!

The fate of humanity will soon get its new wings.

You can ask, "What have you accomplished during this time?

Thanks to god, if somehow you have at least not lost anything.

Let's go and move on,

let's go and move on,

after all, this untidy will soon be gone.

39

WEIGHT OF WAIT

by Jagruthi Kommuri

When the weight of wait burdens the heart,
and seems like everything is coming back to start,
When everything in life seems like a questionnaire,
and you find yourself in mess and despair,
When there's no one there who genuinely cares,
and the road you choose is taking you nowhere.

Don't you lose hope my dear friend,
everything, even life will one day end.
All of this mess is what life is,
dare to embrace every little piece,
yet, fighting the battle is most important part,
even when the weight of wait is tearing you apart.

40

LIFE, A YEARNING

by Shradha Patnaik

In summer, I crave for the gloomy skies
fresh cut grass and a few memories to live by
yet here I am, within these four walls
wondering how I let this summer pass me by?

All alone, just me and my thoughts and a promising
melody of nostalgia coupled with lullaby.

Spirited away to a far-off land
I feel happy at once, unable to place it.
If the genuine feeling, fake or real for once
I envy the ones who have made a place for themselves
indeed.

A clear destination is all I need,
a beautiful experience is all I crave, to wear a smile
seeing the missing pieces of the big picture,
would make all those empty summers worthwhile.

Till then I just hope for the monsoon skies
earthly scent of air, to heal the wounds of summer
perhaps I yearn for the serenity of the blue washed sky.

the warmth of a winter sun, a cup of tea and supper
a warm blanket to cover me up and yes, at last
just a handwritten letter to myself with sentences of
promising love.

41

MMXX

by Ben Holdeman

Came out of nowhere
Crept in everywhere
Trembling and scared
Anger in the air
Isolated media glares
Uninformed
Misinformed
Ignorant storm
Burn it all
When embers cease to glow
Let the phoenix show

42

JAILBREAK

by Ujjwal Datta

Yeah, you read that right. Jailbreak. This is a short story of my voyage through my early childhood days in the quest for acceptance, validation and satisfaction. And no, it does not involve me going to jail. Read on.

Have you ever felt the sudden rush of feelings and this strong urge to express yourself to others? And to get their feedback on it? Well, that is the basic background of most of the teenage peeps. Mine too, for some time, was the same thing. This is my version of it. I, too, wanted to put myself out there and see what reactions people would give. There is nothing wrong with it. It's natural to feel the need to get validation from the people you hold close.

But the mistake most people make is choosing the wrong people to be held close to them. Which is the same thing I did. I thought these people were my life and their opinion, advice would help me in all ways possible. Well, WRONG.

Being a bright student, I was used to getting compliments for my grades and performance and stuff. But I always felt a void inside me which screamed at me to approach those seemingly "“cool” people for their word. Eventually and seemingly enough, my happiness and sense of satisfaction became based on their opinions and their standard of thinking. It became less of my achievements and more of their feedback upon which my mood depended.

I started to feel frustrated whenever I was not accepted by them, or their perspective of my life didn't match mine. I started feeling mildly depressed. You know when there are those days when it's just gloomy, no sunlight, afternoon feels like the dawn, time slows down. Everything becomes just a formality, Exams, picnics, tours, events, Everything. That is what I felt whenever I was unnoticed.

The everyday sky which used to cheer me up earlier, felt like it had lost its charm. The river near my colony which used to relax me whenever I looked into the bubbling water, just became seemingly stagnant. The clouds which used to show me their shapes and stimulated my imagination and creativity, inspiring me to make something out of my boredom, now just felt dead, just floating around without a soul, emotionless, gloomy. The air became thick and heavy, my senses used to die down. As if the time stood still for me to suffer and wallow in my own sorrow.

Time triumphs everything, even my gusto. This was the jail that trapped me from exploring myself, my mind, my personality. The worst kind of jail is your mind itself.

Never let your brain lock you up, it's fatal. I felt like I was buried alive. Throwing hands in desperation to get out of this coffin. Everyday life felt like a developing eclipse. It started to slow down, to darken the surroundings, covering up my sunlight of hope, slowly. The colour palette around me changed to greyish, black, dark shades slowly.

One thing I knew for sure, this is all inside my head. Being the president of the Physics Club in my school, I was definitely an expert in solving problems. But those usually involved planets, mass, forces, time even, never did they involve influences, people, or feelings. So, I started breaking down my problems to get to the base of it and to uproot them from where they started.

So, I started analysing myself, my choices, my moods but I found nothing of any value. Not that there was nothing wrong with myself, but my basic systems were intact, I still was scoring excellent grades, I still won several quizzes, and still represented my school on various occasions. But then where is the problem? It's still pretty dark, I am still down, WHY??

Finally, I found it. The bottom of my research barrel exposed me to the real culprits of my problem. Guess what, I found those people at the root level of my issues. I thought I should give this a try and eliminate this factor from my equation of happiness.

Voila!! The eclipse started fading. Clouds seemed to be taking various shapes. The river was alive again. The sky was roaring adventures again. Light at the end of the tunnel!? Everything started to fall into place, just like I expected. It's so similar to physics and mathematics, take out the toxic and wrong factors, and the solution pops up automatically. I felt great again, felt like my substance which seemed lost, had returned inside me, amazing!

The eclipse which was blocking the sun rays was fading away, paving the way for the sunlight of hope into my life. Colour palettes returned to fresh, colourful, lively ones. I learnt my lesson then and there. Never outsource your own happiness. Create your own game of life and ace it every time.

Create your own happiness. Life is very short and it's not affordable to live someone else's perspective. Your perception is the best one for you, that is the reason it is yours. Build yourself on your terms, never let someone else change a thing or too.

The moment you forget your own self-worth, is the moment you die. If you are a sentient being, you deserve respect and freedom, never take that away from yourself. On the other hand, don't judge someone for their opinions, it's their perspective, becomes subjective.

Well, this lesson came at a price though, 6 months of my life were invested in order to receive this paradigm of self-realisation. But the wisdom which I gained, will stay with me for the rest of my life. I hope this short story makes you feel your inner substance.

Remember, YOLO.

43

OUR OWN SELF

by Jagruthi Kommuri

I searched for someone special, who can be my own,
to love them very deeply and call them my home.
I searched and searched but couldn't find any,
as everyone was special and there were many.
A person can never be other's home this I understood,
cause everyone is their own and enough for their good.
These feelings we have of being lonely and alone
are just mere thoughts that's blurring the reality
cause we've always been our own and individually whole,
the person we find in others is nothing but our own soul.

44

STANDING ON A CLIFF

by Saba Shaikh

Standing on the brink of the cliff
ready to end my life,
you think I will be happy with my own fight?

Jumping off the cliff,
or running for my life
which one will be great?

Anyways, they won't leave me alive
my heart is filled with grief
the grief inside me hurts, like a stinging knife
stabbing my soul
and putting all my dreams aside.
no problem is big and life isn’t so small
everything will be fine
and it wouldn’t stay for long.

I know what I am doing is wrong
but it isn't me, it's my demons helping me to go on.

45

SHORT CIRCUITS OF INNER LIFE

by Jaykumar Patel

Climbing the steps of the inner footsteps,
seems fearful with - open but closed eyes.
From junction to junction when the circuits seem to be complete,
we get confused with the meaning of "short circuits".
You never know, where you would finally end up,
but the thought of setbacks might never lead you to get up!
If sometimes you flew and get drowned in muddy island,
If you chose to try again, then thank you very much.
Dear friend,
do you know where nature's point is?
Where, everything is white and everything is crystalline?
If you endure with your will,
please take me too with you!
We would sail and fail together

and possibly will enjoy the Caribbean gold!

It's very generous to the surroundings, when we forget ourselves from its amazements.

But,

we will surely find that inner in you,

such that it brings you to the point where you can easily fly without any due!

46

WHY DON'T THEY SEE IT?

by Siddiqua Fatima

The amount of awareness that we have online about toxic behaviour is actually quite impressive. I'm glad we have so many people talking about things that have so long been ignored.

I am glad that there's help for those who are able to reach out. I appreciate that these things help people recognise toxicity in their lives and encourage them to move on. I'm glad for all of it.

Things aren't always that easy as it looks. Recognising toxic behaviour can take years. When a person knows what toxic behaviour looks like when they know how it works and how it plays out in any relation with such a person, not because a person is blindly in love or all those cliché things people often think, but because sometimes a toxic person can sell their behaviour off by being relatable to you. In ways, you would really truly understand and sympathize with. They can make you want to protect them because you understand that their shortcomings come from insecurities, insecurities that you understand.

It all seems very logical and humane and they can make you believe that if you stood up for them more, or helped them cope with their insecurities better or solved all their problems, of course, they would never be toxic again. And they do try, I'm sure they do, after all a toxic person is also a person, with a heart, and they must have some goodness in them, even if this goodness is often unbearably eclipsed by their being toxic. Sometimes they do realise their own toxic tendencies, and they make up for it. They make up for it by caring for you and giving you everything that they are able to provide for you and by being there for you, and they do all this so well you question why you ever thought they weren't nice.

But then there will come a time when you aren't able to "help" them or "be there" for them, because perhaps you have other priorities (which is natural) or because their issue was a perceived issue, something non-existent and cannot be solved since it doesn't exist. How wrong you are for not supporting this person, and how natural it is for them to react to you in a toxic way, depends entirely on how nice they have been to you when they felt like being nice, whether or not you wanted it or needed it then. But that is beside the point. They are nice and you aren't. And you shall suffer from the guilt of wanting to distance yourself from someone who is so very kind and caring. Look at everyone else. Wouldn't they all agree that this person was a true gem, one of a kind, a blessing in disguise? Why is it that you are the only person who can't see them the same way? But this feeling isn't permanent.

You'll like them again once they cool down. After all, it was you who let them down in the first place. And it's not that bad, not all bad. There are good times, too, right?

And this is how the cycle continues. Until one sees that the toxicity comes from this other person and not from themselves. That is when all this awareness helps, until then each one is on his own, wallowing away in guilt because they aren't good enough. Only after one is able to see beyond the advertisements of good behaviour and talks of good intention, are they able to see beyond what their guilt blinds and binds them to.

47

MASS

by Ben Holdeman

Tear stained skies
Blood-soaked lives
Perished goodbyes
Ring through the night
Given to parents' cries
Left to agonize
Temporarily eulogized
The cowardly appointed wise
Point and criticize
While more pain flies
Breaking more lives
Humanity dies

48

PAIN

by Jagruthi Kommuri

They say pain changes things.
It changes people just as there's summer after spring.
If the caterpillar is so comfortable being a caterpillar,
it wouldn't have beautiful butterfly wings.
If the rocks aren't beaten by the sculptor,
they wouldn't become beautiful carvings.
When life is tough with the pain it brings,
remember only when shaken,
sound is produced by strings.

49

MOMENTS OF PEACE

by Shradha Patnaik

The feel of sand in our little hands,
to build those dreamy castles.
From nurturing that little seed,
to watch it grow in the sunlight.
Drawing those lovely landscapes,
with a house and a red roof
is all that is peace for me.

To take a deep breath of morning air,
and walking barefoot on lush grass.
Pink paper flowers fluttering in the wind,
the aroma of mother's kitchen
are all my moments of zen.
Suddenly the world makes sense from my window seat,
so even though I am out of my depth,
The serenity embraced me in its warmth.
It's all that peace is for me.

MEET THE CO-AUTHORS

Ben Holdeman

Ben began writing a few years ago to add a little creativity to his life. What began as a random hobby quickly became a daily source of inspiration and joy. This is the first time Ben has had any of his work in print. Ben is from southwest Ohio, USA.

Shradha Patnaik

She is a daydreaming freelance writer and a design from the east coast city Bhubaneswar. An aesthete/artist by choice, she likes to sketch, design and photograph. Loves to read classics and author every odd story on her mind into pages

Aakriti Jain

"Pen is mightier than a sword" is what she believes. An absolute writer who has been pursuing Bachelor in English honours currently. She has been inking her thoughts and expressing herself. "When it becomes hard to connect to the world, writing is my only strength which keeps me going," she says.

Nandish Bhayani

An ecstatic technology enthusiast that has a soft corner for art and poetry. Fascinated by movies, TV shows and a bunch of sports. Trying to frame his feelings and express a different side of his using words assembled into poetry.

Siddiqua Fatima Virji

Siddiqua Fatima Virji is a second-year MA Comparative Literature student from the English and Foreign Languages University, Hyderabad. She completed her under-grad in Literature, Psychology and Political Science from St. Francis College for Women, Hyderabad. She is an enthusiastic reader and writes mostly for her WordPress blog, 'An Unstable Extravert.'

Shravastee Bhattacharya

Shravastee Bhattacharya is an aspirant writer, reader, and student. She has her major works set on life, nature, and human emotions. Her goal is to spread positivity through words.

Jaykumar Patel

Patel Jaykumar Dipakbhai is a student in the field of Physics. Apart from his studies, he is also a skilled musician and loves to sing and play different instruments. Inspired by nature's beauty and with wings of music and art, his creativity and thoughts are bestowed in his poetry.

Saba Shaikh

Saba Shaikh is an 18-year-old amateur writer who is forfeited in the world of books. During the initial stages of childhood, she nurtured her habit of reading books that have forged her fondness for literature. She believes reading is the souvenir that has aided her to grab a lot of knowledge as well as made her a lot more imaginative. Her love for books and writing is immortal.

Sarthak Khurana

Clad under the identity of a working professional breathes a person who is on a journey to find himself & where he belongs. He calls himself a fitness enthusiast who loves travelling and can never live without coffee. An ambivert by nature, he seeks solace and warmth with his writing.

Chirag Sumesara

Chirag Sumesara is a Marketer and Event Manager by Profession. You will find him lost in the past, present, and future at the same time. A creative writer and overthinker who believes that the world is an enigma that perseverance, compassion, and constant learning can crack.

Christina Choudhary

Christina Choudhary of age 21 is pursuing B. Tech in Biotechnology and is a resident of Lucknow, Uttar Pradesh. Her interest in writing began when she was in grade 8. Putting her thoughts and emotions in writing used to make her feel complete and fill her heart with immense joy and that is how the journey of writing began. She is also an admirer of nature and loves to paint that out on paper. A girl full of aspirations and the courage to fulfil her dreams is what defines her.

Juwairiyah Tariq Sayeed

A high school senior, Juwairiyah Tariq Sayeed, loves penning poetry and flash fiction. She derives inspiration from the wondrous beings hidden in the by-lanes and heart touching occurrences she comes across. She transfigures emotions into beautiful words, speaking to the world through ink. She can be found on Instagram with the handle @flight_of_words.

Pradip Chauhan

A medical Student who is a passionate writer too. He always seeks to learn in everything and is ambitious about spreading happiness. He believes positive thinking yields positive results.

Jagruthi Kommuri

Jagruthi is an E-commerce graduate, currently working and an MBA student, started writing to express her feelings and loves to write to ignite a little hope and faith in the reader. She is a simple girl who finds solace in words and writes to spread love & positivity to the world. She believes kindness goes a long way when communicated through the heart.

Ujjwal Dutta

Hunger for precision and accuracy ignites a spark of curiosity within. That is him, Ujjwal Dutta a 3rd-year medical student, an aspiring writer, a teacher, and a critical thinker. His constant appetite for attention to detail and turning poetic insights into stories is what inspires him to pick up the pen.

Akshata Rai

Akshata Rai is just a fellow human finding her escape in ink-filled words and books. Writing keeps her sane and every breath of hers is a constant scribble and struggle of creating a story, one page at a time.

Riet Dsilva

Riet Dsilva is a 20-year-old collegiate whose creativity finds expression through poetry. She finds the realms of the mind fascinating and writes fondly on the subject. Her poems are conversational in tone dealing with the darkness in life. She is an avid reader and often finds herself lost among the million worlds people create through their writing. She hopes to inspire people to live easier and happier lives.

Iniya Sisodia

Iniya is an engineer who is passionate about writing and books. He admires nature and the way it affects one's life and believes in positivity and hope. He is lives in Hyderabad is very fond of learning new languages.

Aeiknor Kaur

Aeiknor is an optimist living in Delhi. She has been passionate about writing and reading since her childhood. Life and its different shades have always fascinated her and inspired her to pen down her feelings. She writes about life and the challenges it unfolds and the beauty of the living.

Rashi Jain

Rashi Jain is pursuing an under-graduation in commerce, who unexpectedly discovered her love for writing. She has a strong belief in being optimistic about future goals rather than reminiscing the past. Her highest priority in life is to find the answers for "What I want to be?" and "What I want to live for?" This quest is on...

Bushra Tahir

Bushra Tahir belongs to the city of Kanpur, India. Growing up, she was fascinated with arts and literature, the reason she is a part-time crafter and writer. A hardcore Potterhead. She is a happy-go-lucky person who is attracted to beauty, intelligence, and eccentric ideas.

John Jason Thomas

A hardworking student, a passionate writer, John has in him the zeal and love for the automobile world. All of these have thrived a learning experience and makes him put great emphasis on the journey of life. He speaks with fervour and has been a part of theatre and screenplay in school life. He believes this great gift of literary work has made it possible for him to realise the extent of life.

Infinity Zero

Infinity Zero is a poet and a writer living in the charming small town of Assam with her kitten, Eep. Her poems are a testimony to those fleeting moments of absolute darkness creeping in at the midnight hour. Also, she loves KitKat. You can connect with Infinity on Instagram @zero_infinity_zero

Ankita Baidya

A Delhi-girl who loves writing about life and the emptiness it brings along. She is a hopeless reader who is a keen learner too and loves jotting down her feelings. Words are her weapons and she bleeds the human emotions with them, allowing them to flow into her poetry.

Neeraj Bhengra

He is a college student who lives in Ranchi. He loves reading and writing about life around him and his feelings. He started writing back in 2014 and is into philosophy and stoicism. He also likes playing basketball.

Gunjan Makhijani

Gunjan Makhijani is pursuing her majors in Journalism from the University of Delhi. She has passed high school with a science stream and has always been inclined towards writing and elocution. She loves exploring different academic disciplines. A wandering mind, but an avid writer at heart.

Sonali Mistry

Sonali Mistry is a journalist, writer, and poet. She believes in the power of prose more than mere words and aims to create a fair, just society with her pen. She is currently working with the Government of Gujarat at Information Department.